Little Golden Books

Little Golden Books

Little Golden Books

Little Golden Books

Little Golden Books

A GOLDEN BOOK • NEW YORK

Compilation copyright © 2016 Disney Enterprises, Inc. All rights reserved.
Pixar characters and artwork copyright © Disney/Pixar. *Tangled* copyright © 2010 Disney Enterprises, Inc.
Brave copyright © 2012 Disney/Pixar. *The Princess and the Frog* copyright © 2009 Disney Enterprises, Inc.
The movie THE PRINCESS AND THE FROG Copyright © 2009 Disney, story inspired in part by the book THE FROG
PRINCESS by E.D. Baker Copyright © 2002, published by Bloomsbury Publishing, Inc. *The Little Mermaid* copyright ©
1999 Disney Enterprises, Inc. *Cinderella* copyright © 1998, 2005 Disney Enterprises, Inc. *Snow White and the Seven Dwarfs*
copyright © 1999 Disney Enterprises, Inc. *Beauty and the Beast* copyright © 1997, 2004 Disney Enterprises, Inc. *Sleeping
Beauty* copyright © 1997, 2008, 2014 Disney Enterprises, Inc. *Aladdin* copyright © 1992, 2004 Disney Enterprises, Inc.
All rights reserved. Published in the United States by Golden Books, an imprint of Random House Children's Books, a
division of Penguin Random House LLC, 1745 Broadway, New York, NY 10019, and in Canada by Random House of
Canada, a division of Penguin Random House Ltd., Toronto, in conjunction with Disney Enterprises, Inc. Golden Books,
A Golden Book, A Little Golden Book, the G colophon, and the distinctive gold spine are registered trademarks of
Penguin Random House LLC.

randomhousekids.com

ISBN 978-0-7364-3617-5

MANUFACTURED IN CHINA

10 9 8 7 6

a Little Golden Book® Collection

Nine Disney Princess Tales

A GOLDEN BOOK • NEW YORK

CONTENTS

Rapunzel had long, long hair and lived in a tall, tall tower. Her hair was as long as the tower was tall. When Mother Gothel came home every day, she called, **"Rapunzel, let down your hair!"** And Rapunzel pulled Mother Gothel up into the tower.

Rapunzel's hair was **magical**. It kept Mother Gothel young and beautiful.

Rapunzel did not know that Mother Gothel had stolen her from her real parents, the King and the Queen.

Mother Gothel wanted the **magical** hair all for herself.

Mother Gothel never let Rapunzel leave the tower. She told Rapunzel that bad people wanted to take her **magical** hair.

Rapunzel had one friend—a chameleon named **Pascal**.

Once a year, on her birthday, Rapunzel saw **sparkling lights** floating into the sky. She wished she could leave the tower and see the lights up close. They seemed **meant** for her.

One day, just before Rapunzel's eighteenth birthday, a thief named **Flynn** was running through the forest. He had stolen the lost princess's crown. While trying to get away from Maximus, a determined horse from the royal guard, Flynn found Rapunzel's hidden tower.

Flynn climbed up the tower to hide. Rapunzel had never seen another person besides Mother Gothel. Rapunzel thought Flynn wanted her hair. But he didn't. Rapunzel showed Flynn a painting she had made of the **lights** and asked him to take her to see them. Flynn agreed.

On the way, Flynn and Rapunzel stopped in a pub. It was filled with scary-looking men. But they didn't want to steal Rapunzel's hair, either. They were **friendly**.

Maximus and some royal guards found Flynn. One of the scary-looking men helped Flynn and Rapunzel escape.

They ran until they got trapped in a water-filled cave. Rapunzel's magical **glowing** hair helped them find a way out!

But Maximus found Flynn again. The horse wanted
to take Flynn to jail. Rapunzel told **Maximus** it was her
birthday. She asked him to let Flynn take her to see the
sparkling lights. Maximus agreed. Rapunzel's wish was
about to come true!

Flynn and Rapunzel had a **wonderful** day. A little boy gave Rapunzel a small kingdom flag. The kingdom was celebrating the birthday of the lost princess.

The lost princess had the same birthday as Rapunzel!

Rapunzel saw a picture of the King and the Queen holding their baby princess. The Queen and the Princess had **green eyes**—just like Rapunzel!

Suddenly, Rapunzel was swept up in a dance! It was the most **fun** she had ever had . . . so far.

That night, the people of the kingdom lit lanterns.
At last, Rapunzel's wish came true. Overjoyed, she saw the
sparkling lights fill the sky. She loved the world outside
the tower. She loved Flynn. And he loved her, too.

On shore, Flynn left Rapunzel and did not return. Rapunzel was **heartbroken**. She did not know that Flynn had been tricked by evil Mother Gothel. He had been captured and put in jail! Mother Gothel found Rapunzel and took her back to the tower.

Back in her room, Rapunzel realized that she had been painting the kingdom's emblem, the **golden sun**, on her wall her entire life!

Rapunzel remembered the picture of the **lost princess** and the Queen. Now Rapunzel knew why they all looked alike.

Mother Gothel was the only one who wanted to steal Rapunzel's **magical** hair. She had lied to Rapunzel about everything. **"Mother, I am the lost princess,"** Rapunzel said.

Meanwhile, Flynn had escaped and arrived at the tower to rescue Rapunzel.

"Rapunzel! Rapunzel! Let down your hair!" he called.

But Mother Gothel would not let Rapunzel go. Mother Gothel hurt Flynn so badly that he could never, ever take Rapunzel from her.

Flynn still thought of a way to save Rapunzel. He **cut** her hair. Without Rapunzel's magical hair, Mother Gothel withered away. Rapunzel was finally free of the evil woman.

But without her long hair, Rapunzel had no more magic to save Flynn. He closed his eyes for the last time.

Rapunzel cried. A single **golden tear** fell on Flynn's cheek. It contained the last bit of magic left inside Rapunzel. Flynn's eyes opened! He was all right!

Rapunzel went to her real parents, the King and the Queen. After eighteen years of waiting, they took one look at the **green-eyed** girl and knew she was their daughter. Rapunzel had come home at last!

Rapunzel loved her new life. She loved the world outside the tower. She loved her new friends. At last, she knew where she belonged.

And they all lived **happily** ever after.

A princess rises early.

A princess doesn't doodle.

A princess is patient,
cautious, and clean!

Queen Elinor had **many** rules for how to be a princess. Merida, her daughter, hated ALL of them. Only when she was alone did Merida feel free.

Since Merida would be queen one day and she was old enough to marry, Queen Elinor felt it was time to find her a husband.

"Marriage?" Merida wailed.

Queen Elinor and King Fergus invited the oldest sons of three lords to compete in the royal games. The winner would marry Merida!

There was Young Macintosh,

Young
MacGuffin,

and
Wee Dingwall.

Merida did not want to marry
any of them. So she won the royal
games herself!

Queen Elinor was **furious**. Merida was
angry, too. She was tired of always having to
do what her mother wanted. Merida lost her
temper. She **slashed** her sword through a
family tapestry—right between the images of
her and her mother!

Then Merida jumped onto her horse
and rode away from the castle.
   When she came upon a ring of stones, she saw
a flickering blue light. More lights joined it. The
will o' the wisps were forming
                     a trail leading her into the woods.

Merida followed the will o' the wisps to a woodcarver's cottage. But the woodcarver was **really a witch**! She offered to make one spell for Merida.

Merida wanted a spell to change her mother's mind. The Witch agreed to do it and started brewing something in her cauldron. When she was done, she gave Merida a **spell cake**.

Back at the castle, Merida brought
the cake to Queen Elinor. She hoped
it would make her mother change
her mind about the marriage.
Instead, it changed Queen
Elinor into a bear!

Oh, no! What had Merida done?
Years earlier, a giant bear named Mor'du
had bitten off one of the king's legs. Now
Fergus **heard** a bear. He **sensed** a bear.

Right away, Fergus knew a bear
was in the castle!

He tracked it up the stairs,

around a corner,

and down a hallway.

Merida's mother was a bear. Her father was hunting her mother. Merida needed help!

Merida's little brothers led Fergus on a wild-goose chase. The queen got away! To thank her brothers, Merida said they could have any treat in the kitchen.

Uh-oh!

Merida rushed back to the Witch's cottage. The Witch was gone, but she had left a clue: **Fate be changed, look inside, mend the bond torn by pride**. What did it mean?

In the woods, Merida and her mother learned to work together. For the first time, they enjoyed each other. At last, Merida understood the Witch's clue.

"It's the tapestry!" she cried. **"Mend the
bond torn by pride"** must mean fixing the
tapestry would make her mother human again!

At the castle, Fergus spotted Elinor.
He thought she was a wild bear!
"Mum, run!" shouted Merida.
Fergus and the other men chased Elinor.
Merida chased the men. Her brothers helped.
They were bears now, too. They had eaten the
spell cake!

Merida had to fix
the tapestry—**fast!**

The hunting party closed in on the bear and tied her to the ground.

Fergus raised his sword. But Merida stepped in and blocked his blow! She had saved her mother, just in time.

Suddenly Mor'du appeared.
When he turned toward Merida,
her mother broke free from her
ropes. She fought Mor'du—and
won. The evil bear was crushed
by a giant stone.

Even though the tapestry was
fixed, Elinor was still a bear.
Merida threw her arms
around her mother.
"I want you back,
Mum," she said.
"I love you."

At those words, her mother
changed back into the queen!

One day, Merida might be queen. But for
now, there would be no more changes. Elinor
and Merida had learned to love each other just
the way they were.

THE PRINCESS AND THE FROG

When Tiana was a *little* girl, she loved to cook.

"Food brings people together," Tiana's **daddy** always said.

Tiana had a **BIG** dream.
She wanted to own a restaurant
one day. It would have music and
good food—and it would bring
people together, just as Daddy said.

Tiana grew up
and worked
hard.

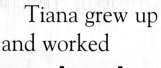

When she had
saved enough money,
she tried to buy a place
for her own
restaurant.

The two brokers
promised to
sell her the
old sugar
mill.

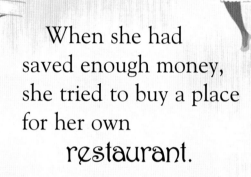

Tiana went to her friend Charlotte's costume party. There the brokers **broke** their promise.

Tiana was so upset that she **fell** and **ruined** her costume. Her dreams of opening a restaurant were gone.

Charlotte gave Tiana
a pretty princess
costume.

But Tiana
was still
sad.

She saw the **Evening Star** in the sky—and made a wish for her restaurant!

But instead of her restaurant, a frog appeared . . .

. . . and **spoke** to her!

The frog said he was really a prince named Naveen. A **bad magic** man had changed him into a frog.

Would Tiana kiss him if he
gave her the restaurant?
NO!

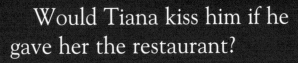

Well . . . maybe one
tiny kiss. . . .
SMOOCH!

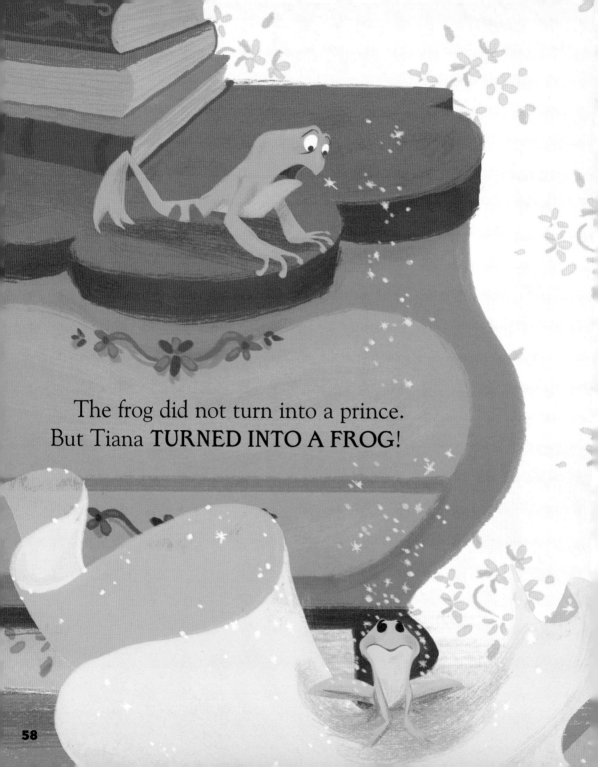

The frog did not turn into a prince.
But Tiana **TURNED INTO A FROG!**

The frogs fell
off the balcony.

They **bounced**
on some drums.

They *flew* away.

The two frogs ended
up in the bayou. It was
SCARY there!

A big **bird**
wanted to
eat them.

Alligators
wanted to eat them.

EVERYTHING wanted to eat them!

Tiana and Naveen **escaped!**

Tiana **worked** while Naveen **played.**

Soon they met an alligator named Louis. Louis loved **jazz**—just like Naveen.

Louis and Naveen **jammed** while Tiana planned.

Soon the frogs were **HUNGRY**. They **tangled** their tongues trying to catch a fly.

A firefly **untangled** them. His name was . . .

Ray and his
family **lit** a path
through the bayou.
The path led to . . .

. . . Mama Odie!

She told the
frogs to find out
what they needed,
not just what
they wanted.

Then Mama Odie told Naveen he had to kiss Tiana's friend Charlotte, who was Mardi Gras princess for the night. Kissing a princess would make both frogs human again!

But the
bad magic
man tried to
stop Naveen.

Uh-oh!
The *chase* was on!
Would the frog
kiss the princess
in time?

NO! Time was up. Naveen and Tiana **remained** frogs.

But they realized that they were in **love**. That was all they really **needed**.

The two frogs got married. Now Tiana was a princess! That meant that Naveen finally kissed a princess.

The magic worked! Both frogs became human again!

Tiana and Naveen *worked* hard **TOGETHER** to fix up her restaurant.

It was the **BEST** restaurant ever! At last, Tiana had exactly what she wanted . . .

71

. . . and exactly what she **needed**—good food and good times with family and friends.

THE LITTLE MERMAID

King Triton, the great sea king, had many daughters who loved the undersea world.

But Triton's youngest daughter, Ariel, dreamed of the world above the water's surface—the world of humans.

Ariel and her friend Flounder liked to go to the surface to visit Scuttle the seagull. Scuttle told them all about the humans' objects that Ariel found at the bottom of the sea.

One day Triton learned about Ariel's trips to the surface. The sea king grew very angry. He asked his friend Sebastian the crab to keep an eye on Ariel.

A few days later, Ariel noticed a ship sailing way up on the surface of the water. She quickly swam toward it.

"Ariel! Ariel! Please come back!" cried Sebastian as he and Flounder swam after her.

When Ariel surfaced, she saw a huge ship filled
with sailors. Ariel's eyes lit up when she spotted the
sailor the others called Prince Eric. It was love at first
sight!

Suddenly the sky darkened. Heavy rain began to
fall, and lightning split the sky. The ship was tossed
on the waves, and the prince was thrown overboard!

"I've got to save him!" thought Ariel. She grabbed the drowning prince and swam to shore, pulling him onto the beach. Prince Eric did not stir as Ariel gently touched his face and sang him a love song.

Soon Ariel heard the prince's crew searching for him. She did not want to be seen by the humans, so she kissed the prince and dove back into the sea.

Prince Eric awoke to find Sir Grimsby, his loyal steward, at his side. Sir Grimsby was happy that Eric was alive.

"A girl . . . rescued me," said the prince. "She was singing. She had the most beautiful voice."

Prince Eric, too, had fallen in love.

King Triton was furious when he discovered that Ariel had fallen in love with a human. He rushed to the grotto where Ariel kept her collection of humans' treasures.

"Contact between the human world and the merworld is strictly forbidden!" Triton shouted.

He raised his magic trident and fired bolts of energy around the cave, destroying the treasures. Then the mighty sea king left.

Ariel buried her face in her hands and began to cry.

Meanwhile, not far away, evil forces were at work in the undersea kingdom. Ursula, the sea witch, who had tried once before to overthrow Triton, was looking for a way to take over. Through her crystal ball she could see Ariel crying, and an idea came to her.

Ursula sent her slimy eel servants, Flotsam and
Jetsam, to Ariel's grotto. There they convinced the
Little Mermaid that Ursula could help her to get her
beloved prince. Ariel was so upset that she ignored
Sebastian's warnings and swam off with Flotsam and
Jetsam to meet with the sea witch.

"My dear," said the witch. "Here's the deal. I'll make a potion that will turn you into a human for three days. Before the sun sets on the third day, you've got to get dear old princie to kiss you. If he kisses you, you'll remain human permanently. But if he doesn't, you turn back into a mermaid and you belong to me!"

In return for the potion, the witch wanted Ariel's voice.

"My voice?" asked Ariel. "Without my voice, how can I—"

"You'll still have your looks, your pretty face," replied Ursula.

After Ariel agreed to Ursula's deal, an amazing change took place. Ariel's voice flew from her body and was captured in a seashell around Ursula's neck. Ariel lost her tail, grew legs, and became a human.

When Ariel went in search of the prince, she was helped ashore by her friends. She tried to speak to them, but no sound came out.

A short while later, Ariel saw Prince Eric. The prince had been lovesick ever since hearing her sing. At first the prince thought Ariel was the girl who had rescued him. But when he learned that she couldn't speak, he knew he was wrong.

Prince Eric felt sorry for Ariel. She needed a place to stay, so he took her back to his palace.

Over the next two days, Prince Eric grew to like
Ariel more and more. During a romantic boat ride,
Eric was about to kiss Ariel when Flotsam and Jetsam
overturned the boat.

"That was a close one. Too close," said Ursula, who
was watching in her crystal ball. "It's time Ursula took
matters into her own tentacles." The sea witch mixed
a magic potion and changed herself into a beautiful
young maiden.

On the morning of the third day, there was great excitement throughout the kingdom. Prince Eric was going to marry a young maiden he had just met!

Ursula, disguised as the maiden, had used Ariel's voice to trick Eric. He now believed that the maiden was the girl who had saved him from the shipwreck.

Poor Ariel was heartbroken.

The wedding ceremony was to take place on Prince
Eric's new boat. Scuttle flew by just as the bride
passed in front of a mirror. Her reflection was that of
the sea witch! Scuttle rushed off to tell Ariel and the
rest of his friends.

Sebastian quickly formed a plan. Flounder helped Ariel
get out to Eric's ship. Scuttle arranged for some
of his seagull friends to delay the wedding. And
Sebastian hurried to find King Triton.

Prince Eric and the maiden were about to be married when a flock of seagulls, led by Scuttle, swooped down on the bride. She screamed in the sea witch's voice.

Scuttle knocked the seashell containing Ariel's voice from around the maiden's neck. The shell shattered, and Ariel's voice returned to her.

"It was you all the time!" said Prince Eric.

"Oh, Eric, I wanted to tell you," said Ariel.

The sun disappeared over the horizon just as they were about to kiss. Ariel's three days were up. She changed back into a mermaid. Ursula grabbed Ariel and dove off the ship.

Thanks to Sebastian's warning, Triton was waiting
for them at Ursula's lair. "I might be willing to make
an exchange for someone better," cried Ursula.
Triton agreed, and he became Ursula's prisoner. She
now had his magic trident and control of the
undersea kingdom.

All of a sudden a harpoon struck Ursula in the
shoulder. Prince Eric had come to Ariel's rescue!
Together they swam to the surface.

Ursula followed close behind them, and she grew bigger and bigger with anger, until she rose out of the water.

Prince Eric swam to his ship and climbed on board. He grabbed the wheel and turned the ship toward Ursula. Just as the sea witch was about to fire a deadly bolt at Ariel from the trident, the prince's ship slammed into Ursula. The evil witch was destroyed!

Now that the witch was gone, Triton was freed. He rose from the sea and saw Ariel watching Prince Eric, who was lying on the shore, unconscious.

"She really does love him, doesn't she?" asked the sea king.

Sebastian, who was nearby, nodded.

"I'm going to miss her," Triton added. Then he raised his trident and shot a magic bolt at Ariel's tail.

The Little Mermaid's tail disappeared, and once again she had legs. Ariel was now a human. Prince Eric awoke in time to see his beloved Ariel running onto the shore. He kissed her, and they were married that day. After the wedding, Prince Eric and Ariel sailed off on their honeymoon to live happily ever after.

Once upon a time, in a faraway kingdom, there lived a widowed gentleman and his lovely daughter, Ella.

Ella was a beautiful girl. She had golden hair, and her eyes were as blue as forget-me-nots.

The gentleman was a kind and devoted father, and he
gave Ella everything her heart desired. But he felt she
needed a mother. So he married again, choosing for his wife
a woman who had two daughters. Their names were
Anastasia and Drizella.

The gentleman soon died. Then the Stepmother's true nature was revealed. She was only interested in her mean, selfish daughters.

The Stepmother gave Ella a little room in the attic, old rags to wear, and all the housework to do. Soon everyone called her Cinderella, because when she cleaned the fireplaces, she was covered with cinders.

But Cinderella had many friends. The old horse and
Bruno the dog loved her. The mice loved her, too. She
protected them from her Stepmother's nasty cat, Lucifer.
Two of her favorite mice were Gus and Jaq.

Cinderella was kind to everyone—even to Lucifer. But
Lucifer took advantage of her kindness.

Lucifer liked to get Cinderella in trouble. One morning, he chased Gus onto Anastasia's breakfast tray. She screamed and blamed Cinderella.

"Come here," the Stepmother said to Cinderella. "The windows—wash them! Then scrub the terrace, sweep the halls, and, of course, there's the laundry."

In another part of the kingdom, the King was
worrying about his son. "It's high time he married and
settled down!" he told the Grand Duke.

"But sire," said the Grand Duke, "we must be patient."

"No buts about it!" shouted the King. "We'll have a
ball tonight. It will be very romantic. Send out the
invitations!"

When the invitation arrived, Cinderella's Stepmother announced, "There's a ball! In honor of the Prince . . . every eligible maiden is to attend."

"That means I can go, too!" Cinderella said.

"Well, I see no reason why you can't," the Stepmother replied with a sly smile. "If you get your work done, and if you can find something suitable to wear."

Cinderella had hoped to fix her old party dress, but Anastasia and Drizella wanted her to help them instead.

The Stepmother kept her busy, too.

Cinderella worked hard all day long. When she finally returned to her little attic room, it was almost time to leave for the ball. And her dress wasn't ready!

But the loyal mice had managed to find ribbons, sashes, ruffles, and bows. The mice had sewn them to her party dress, and it looked beautiful.

The stepsisters shrieked when they saw Cinderella. "They're my ribbons!" "That's my sash!" They tore her dress to shreds.

"Come along now, girls," said the Stepmother. And they left Cinderella behind.

Cinderella ran into the garden. She wept and wept.

Suddenly, a hush fell over the garden, and a cloud of lights began to twinkle and glow around Cinderella's head.

"Come now, dry those tears," said a gentle voice. Then a small woman appeared in the cloud. "You can't go to the ball looking like that. What in the world did I do with that magic wand?"

"Magic wand?" gasped Cinderella. "Then you must be . . ."

"Your Fairy Godmother," the woman replied, pulling her magic wand out of thin air. "The first thing you need is a . . . pumpkin."

A cloud of sparkles floated across the garden. A pumpkin rose up and swelled into an elegant coach. The mice turned into horses, the old horse became a coachman, and Bruno became a footman.

"Well, hop in, my dear," said the woman.

"But my dress . . . ," said Cinderella.

The Fairy Godmother looked at it. "Good heavens!" With a wave of her wand, she turned the rags into an exquisite gown. On Cinderella's feet were tiny glass slippers.

"You'll have only till midnight," the Fairy Godmother said. "At the stroke of twelve, the spell will be broken, and everything will be as it was before."

Cinderella promised to leave the ball on time. Then, under a shower of magic sparkles, she stepped into her coach and was swept away to the palace.

When Cinderella arrived at the ball, the Prince was yawning with boredom. Then he caught sight of her.

Ignoring everyone else, the Prince walked over to Cinderella. He kissed her hand and asked her to dance. They swirled off across the ballroom.

The Prince didn't leave Cinderella's side all night. They danced every dance together. As the lights dimmed and sweet music floated out into the summer night, Cinderella heard the clock begin to chime.

"Oh, goodness!" she gasped. "It's midnight. I must . . . Goodbye!"

"Wait! Come back!" called the Prince. "I don't even know your name!"

Cinderella hurried down the palace steps. In her haste, she lost one of the glass slippers, but she had no time to pick it up. She leaped into the waiting coach.

As soon as the coach went through the gates, the magic spell was broken. Cinderella found herself standing by the side of the road, dressed in her old rags. On one foot, she still wore a glass slipper.

   Her coachman was an old horse again, and her footman
was Bruno the dog. Her coach was a hollow pumpkin, and
her horses were four of her mouse friends. They looked sadly
at Cinderella.

   They all hurried home. They had to be back before the
others returned from the ball.

The next day, the Stepmother told the girls that the Grand Duke was coming to see them. "He's been hunting all night for that girl—the one who lost her slipper. That girl shall be the Prince's bride."

Cinderella smiled and hummed a waltz that had been played at the ball. The Stepmother became suspicious. She locked Cinderella in her room.

Gus and Jaq had a plan to help Cinderella. While Anastasia and Drizella tried to squeeze their big feet into the little glass slipper, the two mice sneaked into the Stepmother's pocket. They got hold of the key, tugged it upstairs, and unlocked the door. Cinderella rushed downstairs to try on the glass slipper.

"May I try it on?" Cinderella asked.

The wicked Stepmother fumed. She tripped the footman who was holding the glass slipper. It fell to the floor and broke into a thousand pieces.

"But you see," Cinderella said, reaching into her pocket, "I have the other slipper."

She put it on, and it fit perfectly!

From that moment on, everything was a dream come
true. Cinderella went off to the palace with the happy
Grand Duke. The Prince was overjoyed to see her, and so
was the King.

Cinderella and the Prince were soon married.

In her happiness, Cinderella didn't forget about her
animal friends. They all moved into the castle with her.

Everyone in the kingdom was delighted with the
Prince's new bride. And Cinderella and the Prince
lived happily ever after!

Long ago, in a faraway kingdom, there lived
a lovely young princess named Snow White.

Her stepmother, the Queen, was cruel and
vain. She hated anyone whose beauty rivaled her own—
and she watched her stepdaughter with angry,
jealous eyes.

    The Queen had magic powers and owned a
wondrous mirror that spoke. Every day she stood
before it and asked:
    "Magic Mirror on the wall,
      Who is the fairest one of all?"
And every day the mirror answered:
    "You are the fairest one of all, O Queen,
      The fairest our eyes have ever seen."

As time passed, Snow White grew more and more beautiful—and the Queen grew more and more envious. So she forced the princess to dress in rags and work from dawn to dusk.

Despite all the hard work, Snow White stayed sweet, gentle, and cheerful.

Day after day she washed and swept and scrubbed. And day after day she dreamed of a handsome Prince who would come and carry her off to his castle.

One day when the Queen spoke to her mirror, it replied with the news she had been dreading. There was now someone even more beautiful than the Queen. And that person was Snow White!

The Queen sent for her huntsman.

"Take Snow White deep into the forest," she said, "and there, my faithful huntsman, you will kill her."

The man begged the Queen to have mercy, but she would not be persuaded. "Silence!" she warned. "You know the penalty if you fail!"

    The next day Snow White, never suspecting that she was in danger, went off with the Huntsman.

    When they were deep in the woods, the Huntsman drew his knife. Then, suddenly, he fell to his knees.

    "I can't do it," he sobbed. "Forgive me." He told her it was the Queen who had ordered the wicked deed.

"The Queen?" gasped Snow White.

"She's jealous of you," said the Huntsman. "She'll stop at nothing. Quick—run away and don't come back. I'll lie to the Queen. Now, go! Run! Hide!"

Frightened, Snow White fled through the woods. Branches tore at her clothes. Sharp twigs scratched her arms and legs. Strange eyes stared from the shadows. Danger lurked everywhere.

Snow White ran on and on.

At last Snow White fell wearily to the ground and began to weep. The gentle animals of the forest gathered around and tried to comfort her. Chirping and chattering, they led her to a tiny cottage.

"Oh," said Snow White, "it's adorable! Just like a doll's house."

But inside, the little tables and chairs were covered with dust, and the sink was filled with dirty dishes.

"My!" said Snow White. "Perhaps the children who live here are orphans and need someone to take care of them. Maybe they'll let me stay and keep house for them."

The animals all helped, and soon the place was neat and tidy.

Meanwhile, the Seven Dwarfs, who lived in the cottage, were heading home from the mine where they worked.

The Dwarfs were amazed to find their house
so clean. They were even more amazed when they
went upstairs and saw Snow White!

"It's a girl!" said Doc.

"She's beautiful," sighed Bashful.

"Aw!" said Grumpy. "She's going to be trouble!
Mark my words!"

Snow White woke with a start and saw the
Dwarfs gathered around her. "Why, you're not
children," she said. "You're little men! I read your
names on the beds," she continued. "Let me guess
who you are. You're Doc. And you're Bashful.
You're Sleepy. You're Sneezy. And you're Happy
and Dopey. And you must be Grumpy!"

When Snow White told the Dwarfs about the Queen's plan to kill her, they decided that she should stay with them.

"We're askin' for trouble," huffed Grumpy.

"But we *can't* let her get caught by that kwicked ween— I mean, wicked queen!" said Doc. The others agreed.

That night after supper, they all sang and danced and made merry music. Bashful played the concertina. Happy tapped the drums. Sleepy tooted his horn. Grumpy played the organ. And Dopey wiggled his ears!

Snow White loved her new friends. And she felt safe at last.

Meanwhile, the Queen had learned from her mirror that Snow White was still alive.

With a magic spell, she turned herself into an old peddler woman. She filled a basket with apples, putting a poisoned apple on top. "One bite," she cackled, "and Snow White will sleep forever. Then *I'll* be the fairest in the land!"

The next morning, before they left for the mine, the Dwarfs warned Snow White to be on her guard.

"Don't let nobody or nothin' in the house," said Grumpy.

"Oh, Grumpy," said Snow White, "you *do* care! I'll be careful, I promise." She kissed him and the others good-bye, and the Dwarfs went cheerfully off to work.

A few minutes later, the Queen came to the kitchen window.
"Making pies, dearie?" she asked. "It's *apple* pies the men
love. Here, taste one of these." She held the poisoned apple
out to Snow White.

Snow White remembered the Dwarfs' warning. But the
woman looked harmless, and the apple looked delicious.

Snow White bit the apple. Then, with a sigh, she fell to
the floor.

Told by the birds and animals that something was wrong, the Dwarfs raced back to the cottage. They saw the Queen sneaking off, and they ran after her.

As storm clouds gathered and rain began to fall, the Dwarfs chased the Queen to the top of a high, rocky mountain.

Crack! There was a flash of lightning, and the evil Queen fell to her doom below.

But it was too late for Snow White. She was so
beautiful, even in death, that the Dwarfs could not
bear to part with her. They built her a coffin of glass
and gold, and day and night they kept watch over
their beloved princess.

One day a handsome Prince came riding through the forest. As soon as he saw Snow White, he fell in love with her. Kneeling by her coffin, he kissed her.

Snow White sat up, blinked, and smiled. The Prince's kiss had broken the evil spell!

As the Dwarfs danced with joy, the Prince carried Snow White off to his castle, where they lived happily ever after.

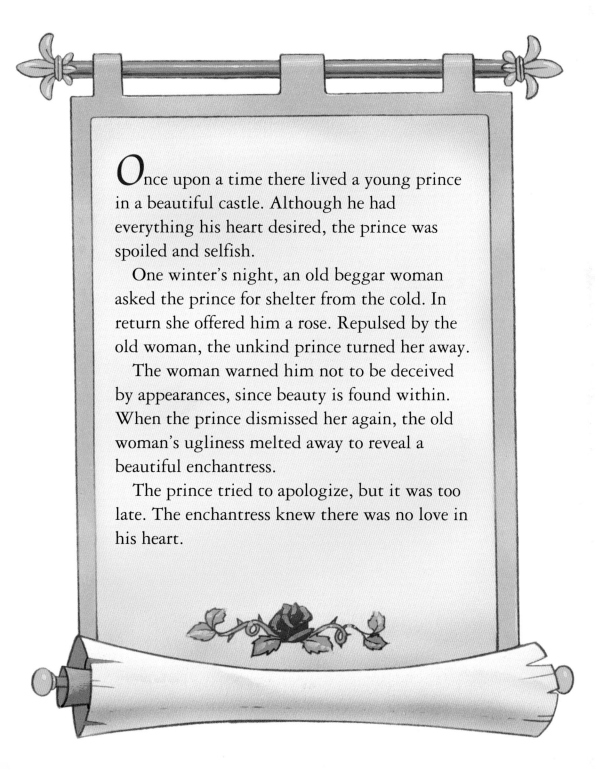

Once upon a time there lived a young prince in a beautiful castle. Although he had everything his heart desired, the prince was spoiled and selfish.

One winter's night, an old beggar woman asked the prince for shelter from the cold. In return she offered him a rose. Repulsed by the old woman, the unkind prince turned her away.

The woman warned him not to be deceived by appearances, since beauty is found within. When the prince dismissed her again, the old woman's ugliness melted away to reveal a beautiful enchantress.

The prince tried to apologize, but it was too late. The enchantress knew there was no love in his heart.

As punishment, the enchantress turned the prince into a hideous beast. Then she placed a spell on the castle and all who lived there.

The rose she had offered him was an enchanted rose. It would bloom until the prince was twenty-one. If he could learn to love and be loved in return before the last petal fell, then the spell would be broken. If not, he would remain a beast forever.

Ashamed of his monstrous form, the Beast hid inside the castle. A magic mirror was his only window to the outside world.

As the years passed, he fell into despair. Slowly the rose began to wither. He did not believe anyone could ever love him.

In a nearby village there lived a beautiful young woman named Belle. Belle, unlike the other girls in the village, cared only for her books. She always felt out of place.

Belle loved to read about adventure and romance. Her father, Maurice, loved books, too. Maurice was an inventor—a genius, according to Belle; a crackpot, according to the townsfolk.

"Belle is even stranger than her father," the villagers whispered. "Her nose is always in a book, and her head is in the clouds."

Gaston, the handsomest man in town, wanted to make Belle his wife. Even though she thought he was a brainless brute and turned him down again and again, Gaston was determined to wed the lovely Belle.

One cold day Maurice hitched his horse, Phillipe, to a wagon and set off to show his latest invention at a faraway fair.

But Maurice read the map wrong and became lost in a forest. As an icy wind whistled through the trees, he suddenly heard the howling of wolves! Phillipe bolted, and Maurice fell to the ground. Trying to escape the wolves, the frightened man ran deeper and deeper into the woods.

He came to a castle and stumbled inside. There he was greeted by Mrs. Potts the teapot, Cogsworth the clock, and Lumiere the candelabrum, who had all been servants to the prince. But before he had time to marvel over these strange creatures, an even stranger one appeared—the Beast!

When Maurice stared in horror, the Beast howled angrily. Then he scooped Maurice up and carried him off to a dungeon.

Meanwhile, Phillipe had made his way back home. Belle took one look at the riderless horse and knew something awful had happened to her father.

"Phillipe! Take me to him!" she cried, leaping into the horse's saddle. Without a pause, Phillipe thundered off toward the woods.

When they reached the castle, Belle burst inside and searched frantically for her father. The enchanted objects led her to the dungeon, but just as she found Maurice, the Beast appeared. Belle let out a terrified gasp at the sight of the hideous creature.

She begged the Beast to free her father. When he refused, she bravely offered to take Maurice's place.

"No, Belle!" Maurice cried, but the Beast agreed to the exchange.

Before Belle could bid her father good-bye, the Beast led her to her room. "The castle is now your home," he said gruffly. Belle was free to go anywhere she liked—except the West Wing.

"You will join me for dinner," the Beast ordered. "That's not a request."

Still, Belle refused, and the Beast stomped off in anger.

That night Belle slipped out of her room and found her way to the forbidden West Wing.

There she saw the enchanted rose by the window. When she reached out to touch it, the Beast suddenly appeared on the balcony outside the window.

Belle screamed and fled from the room.

Her heart pounding, Belle ran out of the castle, mounted Phillipe, and galloped off into the night. But a pack of wolves soon had them surrounded. Belle was helpless.

Suddenly the Beast was there, throwing the wolves aside. Belle heard terrible snarling and howling as the Beast and the wolves battled for their lives. At last the wolves ran off into the woods, but the Beast lay in the snow, badly injured.

Back at the castle, Belle carefully tended to the Beast's wounds. Gentle as she was, the Beast roared in agony.

"I barely touched you," said Belle. Then she saw the look of pain on his face. "I forgot to thank you for saving my life," she added softly.

The Beast only grunted in reply. But when Belle turned away, a hint of a smile appeared on his face.

In the days that followed, the Beast tried to be a proper host. He showed Belle his library, and she began to teach him how to act like a gentleman.

"Perhaps it isn't too late," Cogsworth whispered to Mrs. Potts and her son, Chip the teacup. "If Belle could only love the Beast, this dreadful spell might yet be broken."

Before long, Belle thought of the Beast as her dearest friend. And the Beast thought of little but the beautiful Belle.

One night while she was teaching him to dance, the Beast asked, "Belle, are you happy here—with me?"

"Yes," she said without hesitation. But the Beast saw a trace of sadness in her eyes. Then Belle added, "If only I could see my father again, even for a minute."

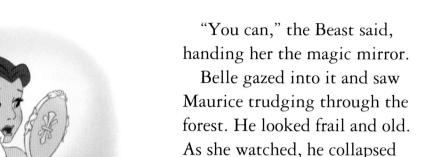

"You can," the Beast said, handing her the magic mirror.

Belle gazed into it and saw Maurice trudging through the forest. He looked frail and old. As she watched, he collapsed in a heap.

"I must go to him!" Belle cried. "He might be dying!"

"I release you," the Beast said sadly. "But take the mirror. Then you will always have a way to look back and remember me."

   With the magic mirror to guide her, Belle soon found
her father and brought him home. But their happy
reunion was cut short by a pounding on their cottage
door. The townspeople had come to take Maurice away.
   Gaston's friend LeFou stepped forward. "Maurice has
been raving that you were imprisoned by a hideous beast,"
he said. "Only a crazy man would tell such a tale."

"But it's true," Belle protested. Her worried eyes searched the angry crowd and fell on Gaston. "Gaston!" she cried. "You know my father isn't crazy. Tell them."

Gaston whispered to Belle that he might be able to calm the crowd—if she promised to marry him.

"Never!" Belle exclaimed. "And my father is not crazy. There really is a beast, and I can prove it." She turned to the crowd. "Look in this mirror and see."

The townspeople looked at the Beast in the magic mirror and grew frightened.

"We must hunt down this savage animal!" Gaston cried.

After locking Belle and her father in the cellar of the cottage, the villagers rode off to storm the Beast's castle.

Luckily, little Chip had stowed away in Belle's saddlebag. After the villagers were gone, he used Maurice's latest invention to release Belle and Maurice from the cellar.

By the time Belle reached the castle, the townspeople had broken in. Gaston and the Beast were fighting on the castle roof. The Beast managed to knock Gaston's weapon from his hand. There was nothing to stop him from killing Gaston.

Gaston screamed for mercy, and the Beast turned away from his enemy. Then Belle watched helplessly as Gaston plunged a knife into the Beast's back.

The Beast roared in pain. Backing away from the wounded Beast, Gaston lost his footing and fell off the roof into the fog below.

Belle rushed to the Beast's side.

"You came back," the Beast said weakly. "At least I can see you one last time."

"No! No!" Belle said, sobbing as she kissed his cheek. "Please don't die. . . . I love you."

At that moment the spell was broken. In one magical instant, the Beast turned back into a prince, and the enchanted servants returned to their human forms.

The castle came to life with rejoicing. There was no doubt that the loving couple would live happily ever after.

*I*n a faraway land, long ago, King Stefan and his fair queen wished for a child. At last a daughter was born, and they named her Aurora.

To honor the baby princess, the king held a great feast. Nobles and peasants, knights and their ladies— everyone flocked joyfully to the castle.

King Stefan welcomed his good friend King Hubert
to the feast. King Hubert had brought his young son
Phillip with him. The kings agreed that someday
Phillip and Aurora would be married.

Among the guests were three good fairies, Flora, Fauna, and Merryweather. Each of these magic beings wished to bless the infant with a gift.

Waving her wand, Flora chanted, "My gift shall be the gift of Beauty."

"My gift," said Fauna, "shall be the gift of Song."

Merryweather's turn was next. But before she could speak, the castle doors flew open.

Lightning flashed. Thunder rumbled. A tiny flame appeared and grew quickly into the form of the evil fairy Maleficent. Her pet black raven was perched on her shoulder.

Maleficent was furious, for she hadn't been invited to the feast. Now she took revenge.

"I, too, shall bestow a gift on the child," she said with a sneer. "The princess shall indeed grow in grace and beauty. But before the sun sets on her sixteenth birthday, she shall prick her finger on the spindle of a spinning wheel . . . and die!"

With a cruel laugh, the evil fairy vanished. Everyone in the room was grief-stricken.

    But Merryweather still had a gift to give, and she
tried to undo Maleficent's curse. She said to the infant:
      "If through this wicked witch's trick
      A spindle should your finger prick,
      Not in death, but just in sleep
      The fateful prophecy you'll keep,
      And from this slumber you shall wake
      When True Love's Kiss the spell shall break."

King Stefan ordered that every spinning wheel in the land be burned.

But he still feared the evil fairy's curse, so the good fairies hatched a plan. They would take Aurora to live with them deep in the woods, safe from Maleficent.

The king and queen agreed. They watched with
heavy hearts as the fairies hurried from the castle,
carrying the baby princess.

To guard their secret, the fairies disguised themselves as peasant women and changed Aurora's name to Briar Rose. The years passed quietly, and Briar Rose grew into a beautiful young woman.

At last the princess reached her sixteenth birthday. Planning a surprise, the fairies sent her out to pick berries. Fauna baked a cake for her, while Flora and Merryweather sewed her a new gown.

In a mossy glen, Briar Rose danced and sang with
her friends, the birds and animals. She told them of her
beautiful dream about meeting a tall, handsome
stranger and falling in love.

A handsome young man came riding by. When he heard
Briar Rose singing, he jumped from his horse and hid in the
bushes to watch her. Then he reached out to take her hand.

Briar Rose was startled. "I didn't mean to frighten you,"
the young man said, "but don't you remember? We've met
before." They had met—once upon a dream.

Briar Rose felt very happy. She and her admirer gazed into each other's eyes. The young man didn't know she was Princess Aurora. And she didn't know he was Prince Phillip, to whom she had been promised in marriage many years before.

Back at the cottage, the fairies gave Briar Rose her birthday surprises. Then Briar Rose told them that she had fallen in love.

"Oh, no!" they cried. They told her the truth at last—that she was a princess betrothed at birth to a prince. Now it was time for her to return home. So poor Aurora was led away, longing for her handsome stranger.

Maleficent's raven, perched on the chimney of the cottage, had heard everything. It flew off to warn Maleficent that the princess was finally returning to her rightful home.

Maleficent sped to the castle. There, using her evil powers, she lured Aurora to a high tower. In the tiny room, a spinning wheel suddenly appeared.

"Touch the spindle!" hissed Maleficent. "Touch it, I say!"

The three good fairies rushed to the rescue, but they were too late. Aurora had touched the sharp spindle and instantly fallen into a deep sleep. Maleficent's cruel curse had come true. With a harsh laugh, the evil fairy vanished.

The good fairies wept bitterly. "Poor King Stefan and the queen," said Fauna.

"They'll be heartbroken when they find out," said Merryweather.

"They're not going to," said Flora. "We'll put them all to sleep until Briar Rose awakens." So the three fairies flew back and forth, casting a dreamlike spell over everyone in the castle.

Meanwhile, Maleficent had captured Phillip and chained him deep in her dungeon.

But the good fairies had other plans for him. Using their magic, they melted the chains. They armed the prince with the Shield of Virtue and the Sword of Truth. Then they sent him racing to the castle to awaken the princess.

When the evil fairy saw Phillip escaping, she hurled heavy boulders at him, but the brave prince rode on.

When Phillip reached Aurora's castle, Maleficent caused a forest of thorns to grow up all around it. Phillip hacked the thorns aside with his powerful sword.

In a rage, the evil fairy soared to the top of the highest tower. There she changed into a monstrous dragon. "Now shall you deal with *me*, O Prince!" she shrieked.

Maleficent breathed huge waves of flame. Phillip ducked behind his strong shield.

Thunder cracked! Flames roared around him! The prince fought bravely. Guided by the good fairies, he flung his sword straight as an arrow. It buried itself deep in the dragon's evil heart, and the beast fell to its death. Maleficent was no more.

Phillip raced to the tower where his love lay sleeping. Gently he kissed her. Aurora's eyes slowly opened.

Now everyone was awake. The king and queen were overjoyed to see their daughter again, and wedding plans were soon made.

The good fairies were blissful, too. It had all ended just the way it should—happily ever after.

One night, an evil man named Jafar and his wicked parrot, Iago, were waiting in a faraway desert.

Soon a thief named Gazeem rode up to them and held out the missing half of a scarab medallion. When Jafar fit the halves together, lightning flashed and the medallion raced across the sand.

Jafar and the thief followed the medallion to the
Cave of Wonders. Jafar ordered Gazeem to get the
magic lamp that was hidden inside. But when the thief
entered, he was eaten by the tiger head entrance!

Then the tiger head spoke: "Only one who is worthy
may enter here!"

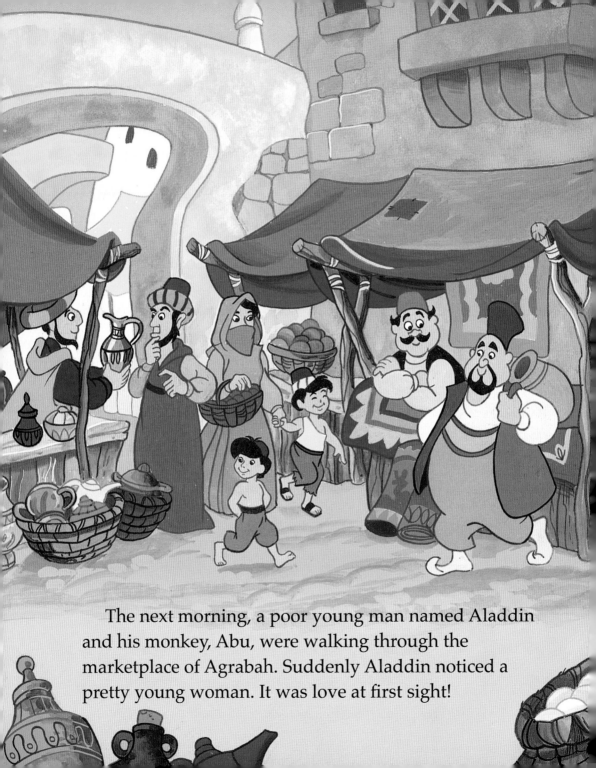

The next morning, a poor young man named Aladdin and his monkey, Abu, were walking through the marketplace of Agrabah. Suddenly Aladdin noticed a pretty young woman. It was love at first sight!

The young woman took an apple from a fruit seller's cart to give to a hungry boy. When the man demanded payment, which she did not have, Aladdin and Abu rushed to help her.

"Thank you for finding my sister," Aladdin said to the fruit seller. He quickly led the young woman away.

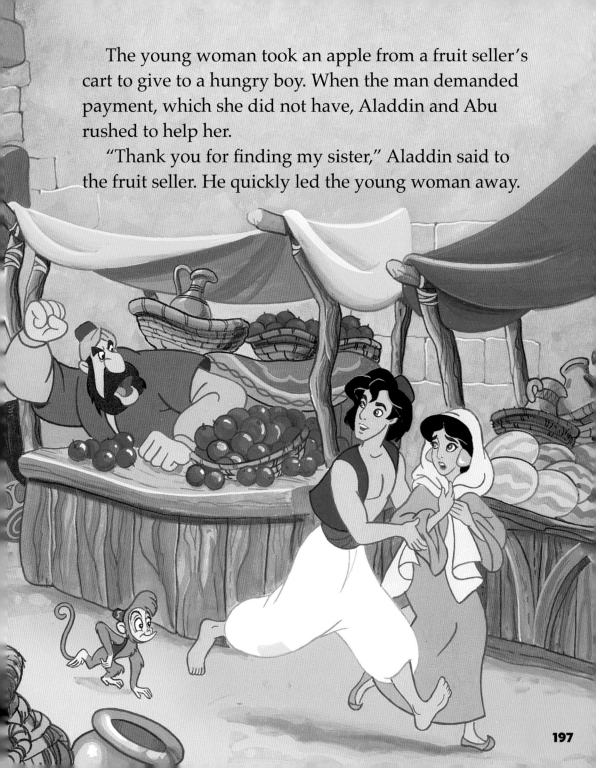

"This is your first time in the marketplace, huh?" asked Aladdin.

"I ran away," the young woman explained. "My father is forcing me to get married."

Suddenly, palace guards appeared. They arrested Aladdin under orders from Jafar, the Sultan's advisor. The young woman demanded that they release him. She was really Princess Jasmine, the Sultan's daughter!

Princess Jasmine returned to the palace and ordered Jafar to release Aladdin. Jafar told her it was too late— the young man had been killed.

But Aladdin was not dead. Jafar had learned that Aladdin was the only person worthy to enter the Cave of Wonders. Aladdin could bring the magic lamp to Jafar!

Jafar took Aladdin to the Cave of Wonders. "Proceed," said the tiger head. "Touch nothing but the lamp."

Aladdin and Abu gasped when they saw all the gold and jewels in the cavern. They even found a Magic Carpet!

But just as Aladdin spotted the magic lamp, Abu touched a huge, glittering jewel.

With a loud rumble, the cave began to collapse. Aladdin and Abu were trapped!

But Abu still had the magic lamp!

Aladdin took the old lamp and tried to rub off some of the dust.

Poof! In a flash of swirling smoke, a gigantic genie appeared.

"You're a lot smaller than my last master," he said to Aladdin.

The Genie whisked them all out of the cave on the Magic Carpet. Then he told Aladdin that he had three wishes.

Aladdin asked the Genie what *he* would wish for.

The Genie replied, "I would wish for freedom!"

So Aladdin promised to use his third wish to set the Genie free. But his *first* wish was to be a prince—so that he could marry Princess Jasmine.

Meanwhile, at the palace, Jafar used his serpent staff to hypnotize the Sultan. The poor Sultan was about to agree that Jafar could marry Jasmine.

Suddenly they heard the sounds of a parade. The spell was broken. The Sultan rushed to the balcony in time to see the arrival of a grand prince. It was Aladdin!

Aladdin entered the throne room.

"Your Majesty," he said, bowing to the Sultan. "I am Prince Ali Ababwa. I have come to seek your daughter's hand in marriage."

The Sultan was thrilled! The law stated that Jasmine must marry a prince before her next birthday—which was only days away.

But the princess did not want to marry Prince Ali. She was not in love with him.

Prince Ali offered the princess a ride on his Magic Carpet, hoping to win her love.

During the magical journey, Princess Jasmine realized that Prince Ali was the young man who had helped her in the marketplace. That starry night, Aladdin and Princess Jasmine fell in love.

Jafar didn't want anyone else to marry Jasmine and foil his evil plans. He was so angry that he had Prince Ali captured and thrown into the sea.

Luckily, Aladdin had the magic lamp with him. He summoned the Genie and asked for his second wish—to save his life! The Genie quickly transported Aladdin back to the palace in Agrabah.

Jafar was determined to marry Princess Jasmine.

"I will never marry you, Jafar!" cried Jasmine. "I choose Prince Ali!"

But the Sultan was under Jafar's spell, and he ordered his daughter to marry Jafar.

Suddenly, Aladdin burst into the throne room and smashed Jafar's serpent staff.

"He's been controlling you with this, Your Highness!" said Aladdin.

Immediately, the spell was broken.

"Traitor!" shouted the Sultan. "Guards, arrest Jafar!"

But before they could capture him, Jafar escaped to his secret laboratory.

As Jafar fled, he noticed that Prince Ali was carrying the magic lamp. The prince was really Aladdin! Jafar ordered his parrot to steal the lamp.

When Iago returned, Jafar made the Genie appear. "I wish to be Sultan!" he demanded.

The moment had come for the Sultan to announce the wedding of Princess Jasmine and Prince Ali Ababwa. A cheering crowd had gathered in front of the palace.

Suddenly Jafar appeared—in the Sultan's robes! The crowd gasped.

"Genie, what have you done?" Aladdin shouted.

"Sorry, kid," said the Genie sadly. "I've got a new master now."

Then Jafar made his second wish—to be the most powerful sorcerer in the world. Jafar the sorcerer lost no time turning Prince Ali back into Aladdin.

"Jasmine, I'm sorry!" cried Aladdin. "I'm not a prince. I can't marry you."

Finally Jafar banished Aladdin to the ends of the earth. When Aladdin found himself a million miles from nowhere, he was glad that Abu and the Magic Carpet were still with him. "Back to Agrabah!" he shouted to the Carpet. "As fast as you can!"

Jafar was in the throne room, enjoying his newfound power, when Aladdin appeared. "How many times do I have to destroy you, boy?" he roared.

"You cowardly snake!" Aladdin shouted.

"Snake?" snarled Jafar. With a loud hiss, he turned himself into a giant cobra.

Looking up at the power-hungry Jafar, Aladdin got an idea. "The Genie has more power than you'll ever have!" he jeered.

"Yes-s-s-s," hissed Jafar. "You're right. I'm ready to make my third wish. I wish to be a genie."

The moment Jafar turned into a genie, Aladdin smiled. Jafar had forgotten that a genie must live in a lamp. In an instant, he and Iago disappeared inside their own magic lamp. They were gone for good!

The Sultan was overjoyed. That very day he changed the law so that Jasmine could marry any man she chose. And she chose Aladdin!

And what did Aladdin do with his third wish? He kept his promise and wished for the Genie's freedom.

"Look out, world!" exclaimed the Genie. "Here I come. I'm free!"